AF306762

Marx Machiavelli Chesterton Emerson Joyce
Defoe Abbott Hardy Montaigne Cooper Austen
Melville Haggard Hugo Grimm
Cooper Eliot
Stoker Christie Molière
Carroll Byron Schiller
Wilde Maupassant
Garnett Engels
Goethe Einstein Fitzgerald Hawthorne Smith Kafka
Cotton Dostoyevsky Hall
Baum Kipling Doyle Willis
Henry Nietzsche
Leslie Dumas Flaubert Turgenev Balzac
Stockton Vatsyayana Crane
Burroughs Verne
Curtis Tocqueville Gogol Vinci
Homer Widger Tolstoy Whitman Busch
Darwin Thoreau Twain Scott
Potter Freud Zola Lawrence Plato Harte
Kant Jowett Stevenson Dickens Burton Hesse
Andersen
London Descartes Cervantes
Poe Aristotle Wells Voltaire Cooke
Hale James Hastings
Bunner Shakespeare Irving
Richter Chambers
Doré da Shaw Wodehouse Alcott
Dante Chekhov Benedict
Swift Pushkin
Newton

 tredition®

tredition was established in 2006 by Sandra Latusseck and Soenke Schulz. Based in Hamburg, Germany, tredition offers publishing solutions to authors and publishing houses, combined with world-wide distribution of printed and digital book content. tredition is uniquely positioned to enable authors and publishing houses to create books on their own terms and without conventional manu-facturing risks.

For more information please visit: www.tredition.com

TREDITION CLASSICS

This book is part of the TREDITION CLASSICS series. The creators of this series are united by passion for literature and driven by the intention of making all public domain books available in printed format again - worldwide. Most TREDITION CLASSICS titles have been out of print and off the bookstore shelves for decades. At tredition we believe that a great book never goes out of style and that its value is eternal. Several mostly non-profit literature projects provide content to tredition. To support their good work, tredition donates a portion of the proceeds from each sold copy. As a reader of a TREDITION CLASSICS book, you support our mission to save many of the amazing works of world literature from oblivion. See all available books at www.tredition.com.

Project Gutenberg

The content for this book has been graciously provided by Project Gutenberg. Project Gutenberg is a non-profit organization founded by Michael Hart in 1971 at the University of Illinois. The mission of Project Gutenberg is simple: To encourage the creation and distribu-tion of eBooks. Project Gutenberg is the first and largest collection of public domain eBooks.

Little Lucy's Wonderful Globe

Charlotte Mary Yonge

Imprint

This book is part of TREDITION CLASSICS

Author: Charlotte Mary Yonge
Cover design: Buchgut, Berlin – Germany

Publisher: tredition GmbH, Hamburg - Germany
ISBN: 978-3-8472-1425-0

www.tredition.com
www.tredition.de

[i]

[ii]

[iii]

LITTLE LUCY'S WONDERFUL GLOBE.

[iv]

"I'm looking at the great big globe that Uncle Joe said I might touch,"
said Lucy.

[v]

LITTLE LUCY'S WONDERFUL GLOBE

PICTURED BY

L. FROLICH,

AND NARRATED BY

CHARLOTTE M. YONGE

AUTHOR OF "THE HEIR OF REDCLYFFE."

*"Young fingers idly roll
The mimic earth, or trace,
In picture bright of blue and gold,
The orbs that round the sky's deep fold
Each other circling chase." —Keble.*

NEW EDITION

New York
THE MACMILLAN COMPANY
LONDON: MACMILLAN & CO., Ltd.
1906

[vi]

New edition September, 1906.

LITTLE LUCY'S WONDERFUL GLOBE.

CHAPTER I.

MOTHER BUNCH.

There was once a wonderful fortnight in little Lucy's life. One evening she went to bed very tired and cross and hot, and in the morning when she looked at her arms and legs they were all covered with red spots, rather pretty to look at, only they were dry and prickly.

Nurse was frightened when she looked at them. She turned all the little sisters out of [2] the night nursery, covered Lucy up close, and ordered her not to stir, certainly not to go into her bath. Then there was a whispering and a running about, and Lucy was half alarmed, but more pleased at being so important, for she did not feel at all ill, and quite enjoyed the tea and toast that Nurse brought up to her. Just as she was beginning to think it rather tiresome to lie there with nothing to do, except to watch the flies buzzing about, there was a step on the stairs and up came the doctor. He was an old friend, very good-natured, and he made fun with Lucy about having turned into a spotted leopard, just like the cowry shell on Mrs. Bunker's mantelpiece. Indeed, he said he thought she was such a curiosity that Mrs. Bunker would come for her and set her up in the museum, and then he went away. Suppose, oh, suppose she did!

Mrs. Bunker, or Mother Bunch, as Lucy and her brothers and sisters called her, was housekeeper to their Uncle Joseph. He was really [3] their great uncle, and they thought him any age you can imagine. They would not have been much surprised to hear that he had sailed with Christopher Columbus, though he was a strong, hale, active man, much less easily tired than their own papa. He had been a ship's surgeon in his younger days, and had sailed all over the world, and collected all sorts of curious things, besides which he was a very wise and learned man, and had made some great discovery. It was *not* America. Lucy knew that her elder brother understood what it was, but it was not worth troubling her head about, only somehow it made ships go safer, and so he had had a pension given him as a reward; and had come home and bought a house about a mile out of the town, and built up a high room to look at the stars from with his telescope, and another to try his experiments in, and a long one besides for his museum; yet, after all, he was not much there, for whenever there was anything wonderful to be seen, he always went [4] off to look at it and; whenever there was a meeting of learned men—scientific men was the right word—they always wanted him to help them make speeches and show wonders. He was away now: he had gone away to wear a red cross on his arm, and help to take care of the wounded in the sad war between the French and Germans.

But he had left Mother Bunch behind him. Nobody knew exactly what was Mrs. Bunker's nation, indeed she could hardly be said to have had any, for she had been born at sea, and had been a sailor's wife; but whether she was mostly English, Dutch, or Danish, nobody knew and nobody cared. Her husband had been lost at sea, and Uncle Joseph had taken her to look after his house, and always said she was the only woman who had sense and discretion enough ever to go into his laboratory or dust his museum.

She was very kind and good-natured, and there was nothing that the children liked better [5] than a walk to Uncle Joseph's, and, after a game at play in the garden, a tea-drinking with her—such quantities of sugar! such curious cakes made in the fashion of different countries! such funny preserves from all parts of the world! and more delightful to people who considered that looking and hearing was better sport than eating, and that the tongue is not *only* meant to taste with, such cupboards and drawers full of wonderful things, such stories about them! The lesser ones liked Mrs. Bunker's room better than Uncle Joseph's museum, where there were some big stuffed beasts with glaring eyes that frightened them, and they had to walk round with hands behind, that they might not touch anything, or else their uncle's voice was sure to call out gruffly, "Paws off!"

Mrs. Bunker was not a bit like the smart housekeepers at other houses. To be sure, on Sundays she came out in a black silk gown with a little flounce at the bottom, a scarlet China crape shawl with a blue dragon upon it—his [6] wings over her back, and a claw over each shoulder, so that whoever sat behind her in church was terribly distracted by trying to see the rest of him—and a very big yellow Tuscan bonnet, trimmed with sailor's blue ribbon; but in the week and about the house she wore a green stuff, with a brown holland apron and bib over it, quite straight all the way down, for she had no particular waist, and her hair, which was of a funny kind of flaxen grey, she bundled up and tied round, without any cap or anything else on her head. One of the little boys had once called her Mother Bunch, because of her stories; and the name fitted her so well that the whole family, and even her master, took it up.

Lucy was very fond of her; but when about an hour after the doctor's visit she was waked by a rustling and a lumbering on the stairs, and presently the door opened, and the second best big bonnet—the go-to-market bonnet with the turned ribbons—came into the room with Mother [7] Bunch's face under it, and the good-natured voice told her she was to be carried to Uncle Joseph's and have oranges and tamarinds, she did begin to feel like the spotted cowry, to think about being set on the chimney-piece, to cry, and say she wanted Mamma.

The Nurse and Mother Bunch began to comfort her, and explain that the doctor thought she had the scarlatina; not at all badly; but that if any of the others caught it, nobody could guess how bad they would be; especially Mamma, who had just been ill; and so she was to be rolled up in her blankets, and put into a carriage, and taken to her uncle's; and there she would stay till she was not only well, but could safely come home without carrying infection about with her.

Lucy was a good little girl, and knew that she must bear it; so, though she could not help crying a little when she found she must not kiss any one, nay not even see them, and that nobody might go with her but Lonicera, [8] her own washing doll, she made up her mind bravely; and she was a good deal cheered when Clare, the biggest and best of all the dolls, was sent in to her, with all her clothes, by Maude, her eldest sister, to be her companion,—it was such an honour and so very kind of Maude that it quite warmed the sad little heart.

So Lucy had her little scarlet flannel dressing gown on, and her shoes and stockings, and a wonderful old knitted hood with a tippet to it, and then she was rolled round and round in all her bedclothes, and Mrs. Bunker took her up like a very big baby, not letting any one else touch her. How Mrs. Bunker got safe down all the stairs no one can tell, but she did, and into the fly, and there poor little Lucy looked back and saw at the windows Mamma's face, and Papa's, and Maude's, and all the rest, all nodding and smiling to her, but Maude was crying all the time, and perhaps Mamma was too.

The journey seemed very long; and Lucy [9] was really tired when she was put down at last in a big bed, nicely warmed for her, and with a bright fire in the room. As soon as she had had some beef-tea, she went off soundly to sleep, and only woke to drink tea, and administer supper to the dolls, and put them to sleep.

The next evening she was sitting up by the fire, and on the fourth day she was running about the house as if nothing had ever been the matter with her, but she was not to go home for a fortnight; and being wet, cold, dull weather, it was not always easy to amuse herself. She had her dolls, to be sure, and the little dog Don, to play with, and sometimes Mrs. Bunker would let her make funny things with the dough, or stone the raisins, or even help make a pudding; but still there was a good deal of time on her hands. She had only two books with her, and the rash had made her eyes weak, so that she did not much like reading them. The notes that every one wrote from home were quite enough for her. What [10] she liked best—that is, when Mrs. Bunker could not attend to her—was to wander about the museum, explaining the things to the dolls: "That is a crocodile, Lonicera; it eats people up, and has a little bird to pick its teeth. Look, Clare, that bony thing is a skeleton—the skeleton of a lizard. Paws off, my dear; mustn't touch. That's amber, just like barley sugar, only not so nice; people make necklaces of it. There's a poor little dead fly inside. Those are the dear delightful hummingbirds; look at their crests, just like Mamma's jewels. See the shells; aren't they beauties? People get pearls out of those great flat ones, and dive all down to the bottom of the sea after them; mustn't touch, my dear, only look; paws off."

One would think Clare's curved fingers all in one piece, and Lonicera's blue leather hands had been very movable and mischievous, judging by the number of times this warning came; but of course it was Lucy herself who wanted it most, for her own little plump, pinky hands did almost [11] tingle to handle and turn round those pretty shells. She wanted to know whether the amber tasted like barley-sugar as it looked, and there was a little musk deer, no bigger than Don, whom she longed to stroke, or still better to let Lonicera ride; but she was a good little girl, and had real sense of honour, which never betrays a trust, so she never laid a finger on anything but what Uncle Joe had once given all free leave to move.

This was a very big pair of globes — bigger than globes commonly are now, and with more frames round them — one great flat one, with odd names painted on it, and another brass one, nearly upright, going half-way round from top to bottom, and with the globe hung upon it by two pins, which Lucy's elder sisters called the poles, or the ends of the axis. The huge round balls went very easily with a slight touch, and there was something very charming in making them go whisk, whisk, whisk; now faster, now slower, now spinning so quickly that nothing on [12] them could be seen, now turning slowly and gradually over and showing all that was on them.

The mere twirling was quite enough for Lucy at first, but soon she liked to look at what was on them. One she thought much more entertaining than the other. It was covered with wonderful creatures: one bear was fastened by his long tail to the pole; another bigger one was trotting round; a snake was coiling about anywhere; a lady stood disconsolate against a rock; another sat in a chair; a giant sprawled with a club in one hand and a lion's skin in the other; a big dog and a little dog stood on their hind legs; a lion seemed just about to spring on a young maiden's head; and all were thickly spotted over, just as if they had Lucy's rash, with stars big and little: and still more strange, her brothers declared these were the stars in the sky, and this was the way people found their road at sea; but if Lucy asked how, they always said she was not big enough to [13] understand, and it had not occurred to Lucy to ask whether the truth was not that they were not big enough to explain.

The other globe was all in pale green, with pink and yellow outlines on it, and quantities of names. Lucy had had to learn some of these names for her geography, and she did not want to think of lessons now, so she rather kept out of the way of looking at it at first, till she had really grown tired of all the odd men and women and creatures upon the celestial sphere; but by and by she began to roll the other by way of variety.

[14]

CHAPTER II.

VISITORS FROM THE SOUTH SEAS.

"Miss Lucy, you're as quiet as a mouse. Not in any mischief?" said Mrs. Bunker, looking into the museum; "why, what are you doing there?"

"I'm looking at the great big globe, that Uncle Joe said I might touch," said Lucy: "here are all the names just like my lesson book at home; Europe, Asia, Africa, and America."

"Why, bless the child! where else should they be? There be all the oceans and seas besides that I've crossed over, many's the time, [15] with poor Ben Bunker, who was last seen off Cape Hatteras."

"What, all these great green places, with Atlantic and Pacific on them; you don't really mean that you've sailed over them! I should like to make a midge do it in a husk of hemp-seed! How could you, Mother Bunch? You are not small enough."

"Ho! ho!" said the housekeeper, laughing; "does the child think I sailed on that very globe there?"

"I know one learns names," said Lucy; "but is it real?"

"Real! Why, Missie, don't you see it's a sort of a picture? There's your photograph now, it's not as big as you, but it shows you; and so a chart, or a map, or a globe, is just a picture of the shapes of the coast-line of the land and the sea, and the rivers in them, and mountains, and the like. Look you here:" and she made Lucy stand on a chair and look at a map of her own town that was hanging [16] against the wall, showing her all the chief buildings, the churches, streets, the town hall, and market cross, and at last helping her to find her own Papa's house.

When Lucy had traced all the corners she had to turn in going from home to Uncle Joe's, and had even found little frizzles for the five lime-trees before the Vicarage, she understood that the map was a small picture of the situation of the buildings in the town, and thought she could find her way to some new place, suppose she studied it well.

Then Mrs. Bunker showed her a big map of the whole country, and there Lucy found the river, and the roads, and the names of the villages near, as she had seen or heard of them; and she began to understand that a map or globe really brought distant places into an exceedingly small picture, and that where she saw a name and a spot she was to think of houses and churches; that a branching black line was a flowing river full of water; a curve [17] in, a pretty bay shut in with rocks and hills; a point jutting out, generally a steep rock with a lighthouse on it.

"And all these places are countries, Bunchey, are they, with fields and houses like ours?"

"Houses, ay, and fields, but not always so very like ours, Miss Lucy."

"And are there little children, boys and girls, in them all?"

"To be sure there are, else how would the world go on? Why, I've seen 'em by swarms, white or brown or black, running down to the shore, as sure as the vessel cast anchor; and whatever colour they were, you might be sure of two things, Miss Lucy, that they were all alike in."

"Oh, what, Mrs. Bunker?"

"Do please sit down, there's a good Mother Bunch, and tell me all about them."

"Why, in plenty of noise for one, and the other for wanting all they could get to eat. But they were little darlings, some of them, if I only could have got at them to make them a bit nicer. Some of them looked for all the [18] world like the little bronze images Master has got in the museum, brought from Italy, and hadn't a rag more clothing neither. They were in India. Dear, dear, to see them tumble about in the surf!"

"O, what fun! what fun! I wish I could see them. Suppose I could."

16

"You would be right glad, Missie, I can tell you, if you had been three or four months aboard with nothing but dry biscuits and salt junk, and may be a tin of preserved vegetables just to keep it wholesome, to see the black fellows come grinning alongside with their boats and canoes all full of oranges and limes and shaddocks and cocoa-nuts. Doesn't one's mouth fairly water for them?"

"Do please sit down, there's a good Mother Bunch, and tell me all about them? Come, suppose you do."

"Suppose I did, Miss Lucy, and where would your poor uncle's preserved ginger be, that no one knows from real West Indian?"

[21] "Oh, let me come into your room, and you can tell me all the time you are doing the ginger."

"It is very hot there, Missie."

"That will be more like some of the places. I'll suppose I'm there! Look, Mrs. Bunker, here's a whole green sea, all over the tiniest little dots. There can't be people in them."

"Dots? You'd hardly see all over one of those dots if you were in one. That's the South Sea Miss Lucy, and those are the loveliest isles, except, may be, the West Indies, that ever I saw."

"Tell me about them, please," entreated Lucy "Here's one; its name is—is Ysabel—such a little wee one."

Lucy had a great sneezing fit, and when she looked again into the smoke, what did she see but two little black figures.

Page 22.

"I can't tell you much of those South Sea Isles, Missie, being that I only made one voyage among them, when Bunker chartered the *Penguin* for the sandal-wood trade; and we did not touch at many, being that the natives were fierce and savage, and made nothing of coming [22] down with arrows and spears at a boat's crew. So we only went to such islands as the missionaries had been at, and got the people to be more civil and conformable."

"Tell me all about it," said Lucy, following the old woman hither and thither as she bustled about, talking all the time, and stirring her pan of ginger over the hot plate.

How it happened, it is not easy to say; the room was very warm, and Mother Bunch went on talking as she stirred, and a steam rose up, and by and by it seemed to Lucy that she had a great sneezing fit, and when she looked again into the smoke, what did she see but two little black figures, faces, heads, and feet all black, but with an odd sort of white garment round their waists, and some fine red and green feathers sticking out of their woolly heads.

"Mrs. Bunker, Mrs. Bunker," she cried, "what's this? who are these ugly figures?"

to see you. Hush, Don! don't bark so!"

Page 27.

"Ugly!" said the foremost; and though it must have been some strange language, it [27] sounded like English to Lucy. "Is that the way little white girl speaks to boy and girl that have come all the way from Ysabel to see her?"

"Oh, indeed! little Ysabel boy, I beg your pardon. I didn't know you were real, nor that you could understand me! I am so glad to see you. Hush, Don! don't bark so!"

"Pig, pig, I never heard a pig squeak like that," said the black stranger.

"Pig! It is a little dog. Have you no dogs in your country?"

"Pigs go on four legs. That must be pig."

"What, you have nothing that goes on four legs but a pig! What do you eat, then, besides pig?"

"Yams, cocoa-nut, fish—oh, so good, and put pig into hole among hot stones, make a fire over, bake so nice!"

"You shall have some of my tea and see if that is as nice," said Lucy. "What a funny dress you have; what is it made of?" [28]

"Tapa cloth," said the little girl. "We get the bark off the tree, and then we go hammer, hammer, thump, thump, till all the hard thick stuff comes off;" and Lucy, looking near, saw that the substance was really all a lacework of fibre, about as close as the net of Nurse's caps.

"Is that all your clothes?" she asked.

"Yes, till I am a warrior," said the boy; "then they will tattoo my forehead, and arms, and breast, and legs."

"Tattoo! what's that?"

"Make little holes, and lines all over the skin with a sharp shell, and rub in juice that turns it all to blue and purple lines."

"But doesn't it hurt dreadfully?" asked Lucy.

"Hurt! to be sure it does, but that will show that I am brave. When Father comes home from the war, he paints himself white."

"White!"

"With lime made by burning coral, and he jumps and dances and shouts: I shall go to the war one of these days." [29]

"Oh no, don't!" said Lucy, "it is horrid."

The boy laughed, but the little girl whispered, "Good white men say so. Some day Lavo will go and learn, and leave off fighting."

Lavo shook his head. "No, not yet; I will be brave chief and warrior first,—bring home many heads of enemies."

"I—I think it nice to be quiet," said Lucy; "and—and—won't you have some dinner?"

"Have you baked a pig?" asked Lavo.

"I think this is mutton," said Lucy, when the dish came up, — "it is sheep's flesh."

Lavo and his sister had no notion what sheep were. They wanted to sit cross-legged on the floor, but Lucy made each of them sit in a chair properly; but then they shocked her by picking up the mutton-chops and stuffing them into their mouths with their fingers.

"Look here!" and she showed the knives and forks.

"Oh!" cried Lavo, "what good spikes to catch fish with! and knife — knife — I'll kill foes! much better than shell knife." [30]

Page 30.

"And I'll dig yams," said the sister.

"Oh no!" entreated Lucy, "we have spades to dig with, soldiers have swords to fight with, these are to eat with."

"I can eat much better without," said Lavo, but to please Lucy his sister did try; slashing hard away with her knife, and digging her fork straight into a bit of meat. Then she very nearly ran it into her eye, and Lucy, who knew it was not good manners to laugh, was very near choking herself. And at last, saying the knife and fork were "great good—great good; but none for eating," they stuck them

23

through the great tortoiseshell rings they had in their ears and noses. Lucy was distressed about Uncle Joseph's knives and forks, which she knew she ought not to give away; but while she was looking about for Mrs. Bunker to interfere, Don seemed to think it his business, and began to growl and fly at the little black legs.

Lavo had climbed up the side of the door, and was sitting astride on the top of it.

Page 35.

"A tree, a tree!" cried the Ysabelites, "where's [35] a tree?" and while they spoke, Lavo had climbed up the side of the door, and was sitting astride on the top of it, grinning down at the dog, and his sister had her feet on the lock, going up after him.

"Tree houses," they cried; "there we are safe from our enemies."

And Lucy found rising before her, instead of her own nursery, a huge tree, on the top of a mound. [1] Basket-work had been woven between the branches to make floors, and on these were huts of bamboo cane; there were ladders hanging down made of strong creepers twisted together, and above and around the cries of cockatoos and parrots and the chirp of grasshoppers rang in her ears. She laid hold of the ladder of creeping plants and began to climb, but soon her head swam, she grew giddy, and called out to Lavo to help her. Then suddenly she found herself curled up in Mrs. Bunker's big beehive chair, and she wondered whether she had been asleep.

[36]

CHAPTER III.

ITALY.

"Suppose and suppose I could have such another funny dream," said Lucy. "Mother Bunch, have you ever been to Italy?" and she put her finger on the long leg and foot, kicking at three-cornered Sicily.

"Yes, Missie, that I have; come out of this cold room and I'll tell you."

Lucy was soon curled in her chair; but no, she wasn't! she was under such a blue, blue sky, as she had never dreamt of: clear sharp purple hills rose up against it. There was a clear rippling little fountain, bursting out of a [37] rock, carved with old, old carvings, broken now and defaced, but shadowed over by lovely maidenhair fern and trailing bindweed; and in a niche above a little roof, sheltering a figure of the Blessed Virgin. Some way off stood a long low house propped up against the rich yellow stone walls and pillars of another old, old building, and with a great chestnut-tree shadowing over it. It had a balcony, and the gable end was open, and full of big yellow pumpkins and clusters of grapes hung up to dry, and some goats were feeding round.

Then came a merry, merry voice singing something about *la vendemmia*; and though Lucy had never learnt Italian, her wonderful dream knowledge made her sure that this meant the vintage, the grape-gathering; and presently there came along a little girl dancing and beating a tambourine, with a basket fastened to her back, filled to overflowing with big, beautiful bunches of grapes: and a whole party of other children, all loaded with as many [38] grapes as they could carry, came leaping and singing after her; their black hair loose, or sometimes twisted with vine-leaves; their big black eyes dancing with merriment, and their bare brown legs with glee.

"Ah! Cecco, Cecco!" cried the little girl, pausing as she beat her tambourine.

Page 38.

"Ah! Cecco, Cecco!" cried the little girl, pausing as she beat her tambourine, "here's a stranger who has no grapes; give them here!"

"But," said Lucy, "aren't they your Mamma's grapes; may you give them away?"

"Ah, ah! 'tis the *vendemmia*! all may eat grapes; as much as they will. See, there's the vineyard."

Lucy saw on the slope of the hill above the cottage long poles such as hops grow upon, and vines trained about hither and thither in long festoons, with leaves growing purple with autumn, and clusters hanging down. Men in shady battered hats, bright sashes and braces, and white shirt sleeves, and women with handkerchiefs folded square over their heads, were cutting the grapes down, and piling them up [41] in baskets; and a low cart drawn by two mouse-coloured oxen, with enormous wide horns and gentle-looking eyes, was waiting to be loaded with the baskets.

"To the wine-press! to the press!" shouted the children, who were politeness itself and wanted to show her everything.

The wine-press was a great marble trough with pipes leading off into other vessels around. Into it went the grapes, and in the midst were men and boys and little children, all with bare feet and legs up to the knees, dancing and leaping, and bounding and skipping upon the grapes, while the red juice covered their brown skins.

"Come in, come in; you don't know how charming it is!" cried Cecco. "It is the best time of all the year, the dear vintage; come and tread the grapes."

"But you must take off your shoes and stockings," said his sister, Nunziata; "we never wear them but on Sundays and holidays." [42]

Lucy was not sure that she might, but the children looked so joyous, and it seemed to be such fun, that she began fumbling with the buttons of her boots, and while she was doing it she opened her eyes, and found that her beautiful bunch of grapes was only the cushion in the bottom of Mother Bunch's chair.

[43]

CHAPTER IV.

GREENLAND.

"Suppose and suppose I tried what the very cold countries are like!"

And Lucy bent over the globe till she was nearly ready to cut her head off with the brass meridian, as she looked at the long jagged tongue, with no particular top to it, hanging down on the east side of America. Perhaps it was the making herself so cold that did it, but she found herself in the midst of snow, snow, snow. All was snow except the sea, and that was a deep green, and in it were monstrous floating white things, pinnacled all over [44] like the Cathedral, and as big, and with hollows in them of glorious deep blue and green, like jewels; Lucy knew they were icebergs. A sort of fringe of these cliffs of ice hemmed in the shore. And on one of them stood what she thought at first was a little brown bear, for the light was odd, the sun was so very low down, and there was so much glare from the snow that it seemed unnatural. However, before she had time to be afraid of the bear, she saw that it was really a little boy, with a hood and coat and leggings all of thick, thick fur, and a spear in his hand, with which he every now and then made a dash at a fish, — great cod fish, such as Mamma had, with oysters, when there was a dinner-party.

Into them went his spear, up came the poor fish, and was strung with some others on a string the boy carried. Lucy crept up as well as she could on the slippery ice, and the little Esquimaux stared at her with a kind of stupid surprise.

Page 47.

[47] "Is that the way you get fish?" she asked.

"Yes, and seals; Father gets them," he said.

"Oh, what's that, swimming out there?"

"That's a white bear," he said, coolly; "we had better get home."

Lucy thought so indeed; only where was home? that puzzled her. However, she trotted along by the side of her companion, and presently came to what might have been an enormous snowball, but there was a hole in it. Yes, it was hollow; and as her companion made for the opening, she saw more little stout figures rolled up in furs inside. Then she perceived that it was a house built up of blocks of snow, arranged so as to make the shape of a beehive, all frozen together, and with a window of ice. It made her shiver to think of going in, but she thought the white bear might come after her, and in she went. Even her little head had to bend under the low door-way, and behold it was the very closest, stuffiest, if not the hottest place she had ever been in! There was a kind of [48] lamp burning in the hut; that is, a wick was floating in some oil, but there was no glass, such as Lucy had been apt to think the chief part of a lamp, and all round it squatted upon skins these queer little stumpy fig-ures, dressed so much alike that there was no knowing the men from the women, except that the women had much the biggest boots, and used them instead of pockets, and they had their babies in bags of skin upon their backs.

They seemed to be kind people, for they made room by their lamp for the little girl, and asked her where she had been wrecked, and then one of the women cut off a great lump of raw something—was it a walrus, with that round head and big tusks?—and held it up to her; and when Lucy shook her head and said, "No, thank you," as civilly as she could, the woman tore it in two, and handed a lump over her shoulder to her baby, who began to gnaw it. Then her first friend, the little boy, hoping to please her better, offered her some drink. Ah! [49] it was oil, just like the oil that was burning in the lamp!—horrid train-oil from the whales! She could not help shaking her head, so much that she woke herself up!

[50]

CHAPTER V

TYROL.

"Suppose and suppose I could see where that dear little black chamois horn came from! But Mother Bunch can't tell me about that I'm afraid, for she always went by sea, and here's the Tyrol without one bit of sea near it. It's just one of the strings to the great knot of mountains that tie Europe up in the middle. Oh! what is a mountain like?"

Then suddenly came on Lucy's ears a loud blast like a trumpet; another answered it farther off, another fainter still, and as she started up she found she was standing on a little shelf of [51] green grass with steep slopes of stones and rock above, below, and around her; and rising up all round huge, tall hills, their smooth slopes green and grassy, but in the steep places, all steep, stern cliff and precipice, and as they were seen further away they were of a beautiful purple, like a thunder-cloud. Close to Lucy grew blue gentians like those in Mamma's garden, and Alpine roses, and black orchises; but she did not know how to come down, and was getting rather frightened when a clear little voice said, "Little lady, have you lost your way? Wait till the evening hymn is over, and I'll come and help you;" and then Lucy stood and listened, while from all the peaks whence the horns had been blown there came the strong sweet sound of an evening hymn, all joining together, while there arose distant echoes of others farther away. When it was over, one shout of "Jodel" echoed from each point, and then all was still except for the tinkling of a little cow-bell. "That's the way we wish each [52] other good night," said the little girl, as the shadows mounted high on the tops of the mountains, leaving them only peaks of rosy light. "Now come to the châlet, and sister Rose will give you some milk."

Page 52.

"Help me. I'm afraid," said Lucy.

"That is nothing," said the mountain maiden springing up to her like a kid, in spite of her great heavy shoes; "you should see the places Father and Seppel climb when they hunt the chamois."

"What is your name?" asked Lucy, who much liked the looks of her little companion in her broad straw hat, with a bunch of Alpine roses in it, her thick striped frock, and white body and sleeves, braced with black ribbon; it was such a pleasant, fresh, open face, with such rosy cheeks and kindly blue eyes, that Lucy felt quite at home.

"I am little Katherl. This is the first time I have come up with Rose to the châlet, for I am big enough to milk the cows now. Ah! do you [55] see Ilse, the black one with a white tuft? She is our leading cow, and she knows it, the darling. She never lets the others get into dangerous places they cannot come off; she leads them home, at a sound of the horn; and when we go back to the village, she will lead the herd with a nosegay on the point of each horn, and a wreath round her neck. The men will come up and fetch us, Seppel and all; and may be Seppel will bring the medal for shooting with the rifle."

"But what do you do up here?"

"We girls go up for the summer with the cows to the pastures, the grass is so rich and good on the mountains, and we make butter and cheese. Wait, and you shall taste. Sit down on that stone."

Lucy was glad to hear this promise, for the fresh mountain air had made her hungry. Katherl skipped away towards a house with a projecting wooden balcony, and deep eaves, beautifully carved, and came back with a slice of bread and delicious butter, and a good piece of cheese, all [56] on a wooden platter, and a little bowl of new milk. Lucy thought she had never tasted anything so nice.

"And now the gracious little lady will rest a little while," said Katherl, "whilst I go and help Rosel to strain the milk."

So Lucy waited, but she felt so tired with her scramble that she could not help nodding off to sleep, though she would have liked very much to have stayed longer with the dear little Tyrolese. But we know by this time where she always found herself when she awoke.

[57]

CHAPTER VI.

AFRICA.

Oh! oh! here is the little dried crocodile come alive, and opening a horrible great mouth lined with terrible teeth at her.

No, he is no longer in the museum; he is in a broad river, yellow, heavy, and thick with mud; the borders are crowded with enormous reeds and rushes; there is no getting through; no breaking away from him; here he comes; horrid, horrid beast! Oh, how could Lucy have been so foolish as to want to travel in Africa up to the higher parts of the Nile? How will she ever get back again? He will gobble her [58] up, her and Clare, who was trusted to her, and whatever will Mamma and sister do?

Hark! There's a cry, and out jumps a little black figure, with a stout club in his hand.

Page 58.

Hark! There's a cry, a great shout, and out jumps a little black figure, with a stout club in his hand: smash it goes down on the head of master crocodile; the ugly beast is turning over on its back and dying. Then Lucy has time to look at the little Negro, and he has time to look at her. What a droll figure he is, with his woolly head and thick lips, the whites of his eyes and his teeth gleaming so brightly, and his fat little black person shining all over, as well it may, for he is rubbed from head to foot with castor-oil. There it grows on that bush, with broad, beautiful, folded leaves and red stems and the pretty grey and black nuts. Lucy only wishes the negroes would keep it all to polish themselves with, and not send any home.

She wants to give the little black fellow some reward for saving her from the crocodile, and luckily Clare has on her long necklace of blue glass beads. She puts it into his hand, and he [61] twists it round his black wool, and cuts such dances and capers for joy that Lucy can hardly stand for laughing; but the sun shines scorching hot upon her, and she gets under the shade of a tall date palm, with big leaves all shooting out together at the top, and fine bunches of dates below, all fresh and green, not dried like those Papa sometimes gives her at dessert.

The little negro, Tojo, asks if she would like some; he takes her by the hand, and leads her into a whole cluster of little round mud huts, telling her that he is Tojo, the king's son; she is his little sister, and these are all his mothers! Which is his real mother Lucy cannot quite make out, for she sees an immense party of black women, all shiny and polished, with a great many beads wound round their heads, necks, ankles, and wrists; and nothing besides the tiniest short petticoats: and all the fattest are the smartest; indeed, they have gourds of milk beside them, and are drinking it all day long to keep themselves fat. No sooner however [62] is Lucy led in among them, than they all close round, some singing and dancing, and others laughing for joy, and crying, "Welcome little daughter, from the land of spirits!" and then she finds out that they think she is really Tojo's little sister, who died ten moons ago, come back again from the grave as a white spirit.

Tojo's own mother, a very fat woman indeed, holds out her arms, as big as bed-posts and terribly greasy, gives her a dose of sour milk out of a gourd, makes her lie down with her head in her lap, and begins to sing to her, till Lucy goes to sleep; and wakes, very glad to see the crocodile as brown and hard and immovable as ever; and that odd round gourd with a little hole in it, hanging up from the ceiling.

[63]

CHAPTER VII.

LAPLANDERS.

"It shall not be a hot country next time," said Lucy, "though, after all, the whale oil was not much worse than the castor oil.—Mother Bunch, did your whaler always go to Greenland, and never to any nicer place?"

"Well, Missie, once we were driven between foul winds and icebergs up into a fiord near North Cape, right at midsummer, and I'll never forget what we saw there."

And here beside her was a little fellow with a bow and arrows, such as she had never seen before.

Page 64.

Lucy was not likely to forget, either, for she found herself standing by a narrow inlet of sea, [64] as blue and smooth as a lake, and closely shut in, except on the west, with red rocky hills and precipices with pine-trees growing on them, except where the bare rock was too steep, or where on a somewhat smoother shelf stood a timbered house, with a farm-yard and barns all round it. But the odd thing was that the sun was where she had never seen him before,— quite in the north, making all the shadows come the wrong way.

But how came the sun to be visible at all so very late? Ah! she knew it now; this was Norway, and there was no night at all!

And here beside her was a little fellow with a bow and arrows, such as she had never seen before, except in the hands of the little Cupids in the pictures in the drawing-room. Mother Bunch had said that the little brown boys in India looked like the bronze Cupid who was on the mantelshelf, but this little boy was white, or rather sallow-faced, and well dressed too, in a tight, round, leather cap, and a dark blue kind [67] of shaggy gown with hairy leggings; and what he was shooting at was some kind of wild-duck or goose, that came tumbling down heavily with the arrow right across its neck.

"There," said the boy, "I'll take that, and sell it to the Norse bonder's wife up in the house above there."

"Who are you, then?" said Lucy.

"I'm a Lapp. We live on the hills, where the Norseman has not driven us away, and the reindeer find their grass in summer and their moss in winter."

"Oh! have you got reindeer? I should so like to see them and to drive in a sledge!"

The boy, whose name was Peder, laughed, and said, "You can't go in a sledge except when it is winter, with snow and ice to go upon, but I'll soon show you a reindeer."

Then he led the way, past the deliciously smelling, whispering pine-woods that sheltered the Norwegian homestead, starting a little aside when a great, tall, fair-faced, fair-haired Norse [68] farmer came striding along, singing some old old song, as he carried a heavy log on his shoulder, past a seater or mountain meadow where the girls were pasturing their cows, much like Lucy's friends in the Tirol, out upon the grey moorland, where there was an odd little cluster of tents covered with skins, and droll little, short, stumpy people running about them.

Peder gave a curious long cry, put his hand in his pocket, and pulled out a lump of salt. Presently, a pair of long horns appeared, then another, then a whole herd of the deer with big heads and horns growing a good deal forward. The salt was held to them, and a rope was fastened to all their horns that they might stand still in a line, while the little Lapp women milked them. Peder went up to one of the women, and brought back a little cupful for his visitor; it was all that one deer gave, but it was so rich as to be almost like drinking cream. He led her into one of the tents, but it was very smoky, [69] and not much cleaner than the Esquimaux. It is a wonder how Lucy could go to sleep there, but she did, heartily wishing herself somewhere else.

[70]

CHAPTER VIII.

CHINA.

Was it the scent of the perfumed tea, a present from an old sailor friend, which Mrs. Bunker was putting away, or was it the sight of the red jar ornamented with little black-and-gold men, with round caps, long petticoats, and pigtails, that caused Lucy next to open her eyes upon a cane sofa, with cushions ornamented with figures in coloured silks? The floor of the room was of shining inlaid wood; there were beautifully woven mats all round; stands made of red lacquer work, and seats of cane and bamboo; and there was a round window, through which could be [71] seen a beautiful garden, full of flowering shrubs and trees, a clear pond lined with coloured tiles in the middle, and over the wall the gilded roof of a pagoda, like an umbrella, only all in ridge and furrow, and with a little bell at every spoke. Beyond, were beautifully and fantastically shaped hills, and a lake below with pleasure boats on it. It was all wonderfully like being upon a bowl come to life, and Lucy knew she was in China, even before there came into the room, toddling upon her poor little tiny feet, a young lady with a small yellow face, little slips of eyes sloping upwards from her flat nose, and back hair combed up very tight from her face, and twisted up with flowers and ornaments. She had ever so many robes on, the edge of one peeping out below the other, and at the top a sort of blue China-crape tunic, with very wide loose sleeves drooping an immense way from her hands. There was no gathering in at the waist, and it reached to her knees, where a still more splendid white silk, embroidered, trailed [72] along. She had a big fan in her hand, but when she saw the visitor she went up to a beautiful little low table, with an ivory frill round it, where stood some dainty, delicate tea-cups and saucers. Into one of these she put a little ball, about as big as an oak-apple, of tea-leaves; a maid dressed like herself poured hot water on it, and handed it on a lacquer-work tray. Lucy took it, said, "Thank you," and then waited.

"Is it not good?" said the little hostess.

Page 72.

"Is it not good?" said the little hostess.

"It must be! You are the real tea people," said Lucy; "but I was waiting for sugar and milk."

"That would spoil it," said the Chinese damsel; "only outer barbarians would think of such a thing. And, ah! I see you are one! See, Ki-hi, what monstrous feet!"

"They are not bigger than your maid's," said Lucy, rather disgusted. "Why are yours so small?"

"Because my mother and nurse took care of me when I was a baby, and bound them up [75] that they might not grow big and ugly like the poor creatures who have to run about for their husbands, feed silkworms, and tend ducks!"

"But shouldn't you like to walk without almost tumbling down?" said Lucy.

"No, indeed! Me, a daughter of a mandarin of the blue button! You are a mere barbarian to think a lady ought to want to walk. Do you not see that I never do anything? Look at my lovely nails."

"I think they are claws," said Lucy; "do you never break them?"

"No; when they are a little longer, I shall wear silver shields for them, as my mother does."

"And do you really never work?"

"I should think not," said the young lady, scornfully fanning herself; "I leave that to the common folk, who are obliged. Come with me and let me lean on you, and I will give you a peep through the lattice, that you may see that my father is far above making his daughter [76] work. See, there he sits, with his moustachios hanging down to his chin, and his tail to his heels, and the blue dragon embroidered on his breast, watching while they prepare the hall for a grand dinner. There will be a stew of puppy dog, and another of kittens, and birds-nest soup; and then the players will come and act a part of the nine-night tragedy, and we will look through the lattice. Ah! Father is smoking opium, that he may be serene and in good spirits! Does it make your head ache? Ah! that is because you are a mere outer barbarian. She is asleep, Ki-hi; lay her on the sofa, and let her sleep. How ugly her pale hair is, almost as bad as her big feet!"

CHAPTER IX.

KAMSCHATKA.

Whisking over the snow with all her might and main, muffled up in cloaks and furs.

Page 79.

Lucy had been disappointed of a drive with the reindeer, and she had been telling Don how useful his relations were in other places. Behold, she awoke in a wide plain, where as far as her eye could reach there was nothing but snow. The few fir-trees that stood in the distance were heavily laden; and Lucy herself,—where was she? Going very fast? Yes, whisking over the snow with all her might and main, and muffled up in cloaks and furs, as indeed was necessary, for her breath froze upon the big muffler round her throat, so that it seemed to [80] be standing up in a wall; and by her side was a little boy, muffled up quite as close, with a cap or rather hood, casing his whole head, his hands gloved in fur up to the elbows, and long fur boots. He had an immense long whip in his hand, and was flourishing it, and striking with it—at what? They were an enormous way off from him, but they really were very big dogs, rushing along like the wind, and bearing along with them—what? Lucy's ambition—a sledge, a thing without wheels, but gliding along most rapidly on the hard snow; flying, flying almost fast enough to take away her breath, and leaving birds, foxes, and any creature she saw for one instant, far behind. And—what was very odd—the young driver had no reins; he shouted at the dogs and now and then threw a stick at them, and they quite seemed to understand, and turned when he wanted them. Lucy wondered how he or they knew the way, it all seemed such a waste of snow; and after feeling at first as if the rapidity of their course made [81] her unable to speak, she ventured on gasping out, "Well, I've been in an express train, but this beats it! Where are you going?"

"To Petropawlowsky, to change these skins for whisky and coffee, and rice," answered the boy.

"What skins are they?" asked Lucy.

"Bears'—big brown bears that Father killed in a cave—and wolves' and those of the little ermine and sable that we trap. We get much, much for the white ermine and his black tail. Father's coming in another sledge with, oh! such a big pile. Don't you hear his dogs yelp? We'll win the race yet! Ugh! hoo! hoo! hoo-o-o!—On! on! lazy ones, on, I say! don't let the old dogs catch the young!"

Crack, crack, went the whip; the dogs yelped with eagerness,— they don't bark, those Northern dogs; the little Kamschatkadale bawled louder and louder, and never saw when Lucy rolled off behind, and was left in the middle of a huge snowdrift, while he flew on with his load. [82]

Here were his father's dogs overtaking her; picking her—some one picking her up. No, it was Don! and here was Mrs. Bunker exclaiming, "Well, I never thought to find Miss Lucy in no better a place than on Master's old bearskin!"

[83]

CHAPTER X.

THE TURK.

"What a beautiful long necklace, Mrs. Bunker! May I have it for Lonicera?"

"You may play with it while you are here, Missie, if you'll take care not to break the string, but it is too curious for you to take home and lose. It is what they call a Turkish rosary; they say it is made of rose-leaves reduced to a paste and squeezed ever so hard together, and that the poor ladies that are shut up in the harems have little or nothing to do but to run them through their fingers."

"It has a very nice smell," said Lucy, [84] examining the dark brown beads, which hung rather loosely on their string, and letting them fall one by one through her hands, till of course that happened which she was hoping for: she woke on a long low sofa, in the midst of a room all carpet and cushions, in bright colours and gorgeous patterns, curling about with no particular meaning; and with a window of rich brass lattice-work.

And by her side there was an odd bubbling, that put her in mind of blowing the soap-suds into a honey-comb when preparing them for bubble blowing; but when she looked round she saw something very unlike the long pipes her brother called "churchwardens," or the basin of soap-suds. There was a beautifully shaped glass bottle, and into it went a long, long twisting tube, like a snake coiled on the floor, and the other end of the serpent, instead of a head, had an amber mouth-piece which went between a pair of lips. Lucy knew it for a hubble-bubble or narghilhe, and saw that the [85] lips were in a brown face, with big black eyes, round which dark bluish circles were drawn. The jet-black hair was carefully braided with jewels, and over it was thrown a great rose-coloured gauze veil; there was a loose purple satin sort of pelisse over a white silk embroidered vest, tied in with a sash, striped with all manner of colours, also immense wide white muslin trousers, out of which peeped a pair of brown bare feet, which, however, had a splendid pair of slippers curled up at the toes.

The owner seemed to be very little older than Lucy, and sat gravely looking at her for a little while, then clapped her hands. A black woman came, and the young Turkish maiden said, "Bring coffee for the little Frank lady."

So a tiny table of mother-of-pearl was brought, and on it some exquisite little striped porcelain cups, standing not in saucers, but in silver filigree cups into which they exactly fitted. Lucy remembered her Chinese experience, and did not venture to ask for milk or sugar, but [86] she found that the real Turkish coffee was so pure and delicate that she could bear to drink it without.

Page 86.

"Where are your jewels?" then asked the little hostess.

"I'm not old enough to have any?"

"How old are you?"

"Nine."

"Nine! I'm only ten, and I shall be married next week——"

"Married! Oh, no, you are joking."

"Yes, I shall. Selim Bey has paid my father the dowry for me, and I shall be taken to his house next week."

"And I suppose you like him very much."

"He looks big and tall," said the child with exultation. "I saw him riding when I went with my mother to the Sweet Waters. 'Amina,' she said, 'there is your lord, in the Frankish coat—with the white horse.'"

"Have you not talked to him?"

"What should I do that for?" [89]

"Aunt Bessie used to like to talk to nobody but Uncle Frank before they were married."

"I shall talk enough when I am married. I shall make him give me plenty of sweetmeats, and a carriage with two handsome bullocks, and the biggest Nubian black slave in the market to drive me to Sweet Waters, in a thin blue veil, with all my jewels on. Father says that Selim Bey will give me everything, and a Frank governess. What is a governess? Is it anything like the little gold case you have round your neck?"

"My locket with Mamma's hair? Oh, no, no," said Lucy, laughing; "a governess is a lady to teach you."

"I don't want to learn any more," said Amina, much disgusted; "I shall tell him I can make a pillau, and dry sweetmeats, and roll rose-leaves. What should I learn for?"

"Should you not like to read and write?"

"Teaching is only meant for men. They have got to read the Koran, but it is all ugly letters; I won't learn to read." [90]

"You don't know how nice it is to read stories, and all about different countries. Ah! I wish I was in the schoolroom, at home, and I would show you how pleasant it is."

And Lucy seemed to have her wish all at once, for she and Amina stood in her own schoolroom, but with no one else there. The first thing Amina did was to scream, "Oh, what shocking windows! even men can see in; shut them up." She rolled herself up in her veil, and Lucy could only satisfy her by pulling down all the blinds, after which she ventured to look about a little. "What have you to sit on?" she asked, with great disgust.

"Chairs and stools," said Lucy, laughing and showing them.

"These little tables with four legs! How can you sit on them?"

Lucy sat down and showed her. "That is not sitting," she said, and tried to curl herself up cross-legged; "I can't dangle down my legs."

"Our governess always makes us write out [91] a tense of a French verb if she sees us sitting with our legs crossed," said Lucy, laughing with much amusement at Amina's attempts to wriggle herself up on the stool whence she nearly fell.

"Ah, I will never have a governess!" cried Amina. "I will cry, and cry, and give Selim Bey no rest till he promises to let me alone. What a dreadful place this is! Where can you sleep?"

"In bed, to be sure" said Lucy.

"I see no cushions to lie on."

"No; we have bedrooms, and beds there. We should not think of taking off our clothes here."

"What should you undress for?"

"To sleep, of course."

"How horrible! We sleep in all our clothes wherever we like to lie down. We never undress but for the bath. Do you go to the bath?"

"I have a bath every morning, when I get up, in my own room." [92]

"I will show you where you live. This is Constantinople."

Page 92.

"Bathe at home! Then you never see your friends? We meet at the bath, and talk and play and laugh."

"Meet bathing! No, indeed! We meet at home, and out of doors," said Lucy; "my friend Annie and I walk together."

"Walk together! what, in the street? Shocking! You cannot be a lady."

"Indeed I am," said Lucy, colouring up. "My Papa is a gentleman. And see how many books we have, and how much we have to learn! French, and music, and sums, and grammar, and history, and geography."

"I *will* not be a Frank! No, no! I will not learn," said the alarmed Amina on hearing this catalogue poured forth.

"Geography is very nice," said Lucy; "here are our maps. I will show you where you live. This is Constantinople."

"I live at Stamboul," said Amina, scornfully.

"There is Stamboul in little letters below — look." [95]

"That Stamboul! The Frank girl is false; Stamboul is a large, large, beautiful place; not a little black speck. I can see it from my lattice. White houses and mosques in the sun, and the blue Golden Horn, with the little caiques gliding."

Before Lucy could explain, the door opened, and one of her brothers put in his head. At once Amina began to scream and roll herself in the window curtain. "A man in the harem! Oh! oh! oh! Were there no slippers at the door?" And her screaming brought Lucy awake at Uncle Joe's again.

[96]

CHAPTER XI.

SWITZERLAND.

"I liked the mountain girl best of all," thought Lucy. "I wonder whether I shall ever get among the mountains again. There's a great stick in the corner that Uncle Joe calls his alpenstock. I'll go and read the names upon it. They are all the mountains where he has used it."

She read Mount Blanc, Mount Cenis, the Wengern, and so on; and of course as she read and sung them over to herself, they lulled her off into her wonderful dreams, and brought her this time into a meadow, steep and sloping, but full of flowers, the loveliest flowers, of all kinds, growing among the long grass that [97] waved over them. The fresh clear air was so delicious that she almost hoped she was gone back to her dear Tyrol; but the hills were not the same.

She saw upon the slope quantities of cows, goats, and sheep, feeding just as on the Tyrolese Alps; but beyond was a dark row of pines, and up above, in the sky as it were, rose all round great sharp points—like clouds for their whiteness, but not in their straight jagged outlines; and here and there the deep grey clefts between seemed to spread into white rivers, or over the ruddy purple of the half-distance came sharp white lines darting downwards.

As she sat up in the grass and looked about her, a bark startled her. A dog began to growl, bark, and dance round her, so that she would have been much frightened if the next moment a voice had not called him off—"Fie, Brilliant, down; let the little girl alone. *Fi donc.* He is good, Mademoiselle, never fear. He helps me keep the cows." [98]

"I cut it out with my knife, all myself."

"Who are you, then?"

"I am Maurice, the little herd-boy. I live with my grandmother, and work for her."

"What, in keeping cows?"

"Yes; and look here!"

"O the delicious little cottage! It has eaves, and windows, and balconies, and a door, and little cows and sheep, and men and women, all in pretty white wood! You did not make it, Maurice?"

"Yes, truly, I did; I cut it out with my knife, all myself."

"How clever you must be. And what shall you do with it?"

"I shall watch for a carriage with ladies winding up that long road; and then I shall stand and take off my hat, and hold out my cottage. Perhaps they will buy it, and then I shall have enough to get grandmother a warm gown for the winter. When I grow bigger I will be a guide, like my father."

"A guide?" [101]

"Yes, to lead travellers up to the mountain-tops. There is nowhere you English will not go. The harder a mountain is to climb, the more bent you are on going up. And oh, I shall love it too! There are the great glaciers, the broad streams of ice that fill up the furrows of the mountains, with the crevasses so blue and beautiful and cruel. It was in one of them my father was swallowed up."

"Ah! then how can you love them?" said Lucy.

"Because they are so grand and so beautiful," said Maurice. "No other place has the like, and they make one's heart swell with wonder, and joy in the God who made them. And it is only the brave who dare to climb them!"

And Maurice's eyes sparkled, and Lucy looked at the clear, stern glory of the mountain points, and felt as if she understood him.

[102]

CHAPTER XII.

THE COSSACK.

While he jerked out his arms and legs as if they were pulled by strings.

Page 102.

Caper, caper; dance, dance. What a wonderful dance it was, just as if the little fellow had been made of cork, so high did he bound the moment he touched the ground; while he jerked out his arms and legs as if they were pulled by strings, like the Marionettes that had once performed in the front of the window. Only, his face was all fun and life, and he did look so proud and delighted to show what he could do; and it was all in clear, fresh, open air, the whole extent covered with short green grass, upon which were grazing herds of small lean horses, and flocks of sheep without tails, [105]

55

but with their wool puffed out behind into a sort of bustle or *panier*. There was a cluster of clean, white-looking houses in the distance; and Lucy knew that she was in the great plains called the Steppes, that lie between the rivers Volga and Don, and may be either in Europe or Asia, according as you look at an old map or a new.

"Do you live there?" she asked, by way of beginning the conversation.

"Yes; my father is the hetman of the Stantitza, and these are my holidays. I go to school at Tcherkask most part of the year."

"Tcherkask! Oh, what a funny name!"

"And you would think it a funny town if you were there. It is built on a great bog by the side of the river Volga; all the houses stand on piles of timber, and in the spring the streets are full of water, and one has to sail about in boats."

"Oh! that must be delicious."

"I don't like it as much as coming home and [106] riding. See!" and as he whistled, one of the horses came whinnying up, and put his nose over the boy's shoulder.

"Good fellow! But your horses are thin; they look little."

"Little!" cried the young Cossack. "Why, do you know what our little horses can do? There are not many armies in Europe that they have not ridden down, at one time or another. Why, the church at Tcherkask is hung all round with Colours we have taken from our enemies. There's the Swede—didn't Charles XII. get the worst of it when he came in his big boots after the Cossack?—ay, and the Turk, and the Austrian, and the German, and the French? Ah! doesn't my grandfather tell how he rode his good little horse all the way from the Volga to the Seine, and the good Czar Alexander himself gave him the medal with 'Not unto us, but unto Thy Name be the praise'? Our father the Czar does not think so little of us and our horses as you do, young lady." [107]

"I beg your pardon," said Lucy; "I did not know what your horses could do."

"Oh, you did not! That is some excuse for you. I'll show you."

And in one moment he was on the back of his little horse, leaning down on its neck, and galloping off over the green plain like the wind; but it seemed to Lucy as if she had only just watched him out of sight on one side before he was close to her on the other, having whirled round and cantered close up to her while she was looking the other way. "Come up with me," he said; and in one moment she had been swept up before him on the little horse's neck, and was flying so wildly over the Steppes that her breath and sense failed her, and she knew no more till she was safe by Mrs. Bunker's fireside again.

[108]

CHAPTER XIII.

SPAIN.

"Suppose and suppose I go to sleep again; what should I like to see next? A sunny place, I think, where there is sea to look at. Shall it be Spain, and shall it be among the poor people? Well, I think I should like to be where there is a little lady girl. I hope they are not all as lazy and conceited as the Chinese and the Turk."

So Lucy awoke in a large cool room with a marble floor and heavy curtains, but with little furniture except one table, and a row of chairs ranged along the wall. It had two windows, one [109] looking out into a garden, — such a garden! — orange-trees with shining leaves and green and golden fruit and white flowers, and jasmines, and great lilies standing round about a marble court, in the midst of which was a basin of red marble, where a fountain was playing, making a delicious splashing; and out beyond these sparkled in the sun the loveliest and most delicious of blue seas — the same blue sea, indeed, that Lucy had seen in her Italian visit.

That window was empty; but the other, which looked out into the street, had cushions laid on the sill, an open-work stone ledge beyond, and little looking-glasses on either side; and leaning over this sill there was seated a little maiden in a white frock, but with a black lace veil fastened by a rose into her jet-black hair, and the daintiest, prettiest-shaped little feet imaginable in white satin shoes, which could be plainly seen as she knelt on the window-seat.

"What are you looking at?" asked Lucy, coming to her side. [110]

"See now," cried the Spaniard, "stand there. Ah! have you no castanets?"

Page 110.

"I'm watching for the procession. Then I shall go to church with Mamma. Look! That way we shall see it come; these two mirrors reflect everything up and down the street."

"Are you dressed for church?" asked Lucy. "You have no hat on."

58

"Where does your grace come from not to know that a mantilla is what is fit for church? Mamma is being dressed in her black silk and her black mantilla."

"And your shoes?"

"I could not wear great, coarse, hard shoes," said the little Doña Iñes; "it would spoil my feet. Ah! I shall have time to show the Senorita what I can do. Can your grace dance?"

"I danced with Uncle Joe at our last Christmas party," said Lucy, with great dignity.

"See now," cried the Spaniard; "stand there. Ah! have you no castanets?" and she quickly took out two very small ivory shells or bowls, each pair fastened together by a loop, through which she passed her thumb so that the little [113] spoons hung on her palm, and she could snap them together with her fingers.

Then she began to dance round Lucy in the most graceful swimming way, now rising, now falling, and cracking her castanets together at intervals. Lucy tried to do the same, but her limbs seemed like a wooden doll's compared with the suppleness and ease of Iñes. She made sharp corners and angles, where the Spaniard floated so like a sea-bird that it was like seeing her fly or float rather than merely dance, till at last the very watching her rendered Lucy drowsy and dizzy, and as the church bells began to ring, and the chant of the procession to sound, she lost all sense of being in sunny Malaga, the home of grapes.

[114]

CHAPTER XIV.

GERMANY.

Page 114.

There was a great murmur and buzz of learning lessons; rows upon rows of little boys were sitting before desks, studying; very few heads looked up as Lucy found herself walking round the room—a large clean room, with maps hanging on the walls, but hot and weary-feeling, because there were no windows open and so little fresh air.

"What are you about, little boy?" she asked.

"I am learning my verb," he said; "*moneo, mones, monet.*"

60

Lucy waited no longer, but moved off to another desk. "And what are you doing?" [117]

"I am writing my analysis."

Lucy did not know what an analysis was, so she went a little further. "What are you doing here?" she said timidly, for these were somewhat bigger boys.

"We are drawing up an essay on the individuality of self."

That was enough to frighten any one away, and Lucy betook herself to some quite little boys, with fat rosy faces and light hair. "Are you busy, too?" she said.

"Oh yes; we are learning the chief cities of the Fatherland."

Lucy felt like the little boy in the fable, who could not get either the dog, or the bird, or the bee, to play with him.

"When do you play?" she asked.

"We have an hour's interval after dinner, and another at supper-time, but then we prepare our work for the morrow," said one of the boys, looking up well satisfied.

"Work! work! Are you always at work?" [118] exclaimed Lucy; "I only learn from nine to half-past twelve, and half an hour to get my lessons in the afternoon."

"You are a maiden," said the little boy with civil superiority; "your brothers learn more hours."

"More; yes, but not so many as you do. They play from twelve till half-past two, and have two half-holidays in the week."

"So, you are not industrious. We are. That is the reason why we can all act together, and think together, so much better than any others; and we all stand as one irresistible power, the United Germany."

Lucy gave a little gasp! it was all so very wise.

"May I see your sisters?" she said.

The little sisters, Gretchens and Kätchens were learning away almost as hard as the Hermanns and Fritzes, but the bigger sisters had what Lucy thought a better time of it. One of them was helping in the kitchen, and another [119] in the ironing; but then they had their books and their music, and in the evening all the families came out into the pleasure gardens, and had little tables with coffee before them, and the mammas knitted, and the papas smoked, and the young ladies listened to the band. On the whole, Lucy thought she should not mind living in Germany, if they would not do so many lessons.

[120]

CHAPTER XV.

PARIS IN THE SIEGE.

"And Uncle Joe is in France, where the fathers and brothers of those little Prussian boys have been fighting. Suppose and suppose I could see it."

There was a thunder and a whizzing in the air and a sharp rattling noise besides; a strange, damp, unwholesome smell too, mixed with that of gunpowder; and when Lucy looked up, she found herself down some steps in a dark, dull, vaulted-looking place, lined with stone, however, and open to the street above. A little lamp was burning in a corner, piles of straw and bits [123] of furniture were lying about, and upon one of the bundles of straw sat a little rough-haired girl.

selle, good morning. Are you come here to take shelter from the shells?"

Page 123.

"Ah! Mademoiselle, good morning," she said. "Are you come here to take shelter from the shells? The battery is firing now; I do not think Mamma will come home till it slackens a little. She is gone to the distribution of meat, to get a piece of horse for my brother, who is weak after his wounds. I wish I could offer you something, but we have nothing but water, and it is not even sugared."

"Do you live down here?" asked Lucy, looking round at the dreary place with wonder.

"Not always. We used to have a pretty little house up over, but the cruel shells came crashing in, and flew into pieces, tearing everything to splinters, and we are only safe from them down here. Ah, if I could only have shown you Mamma's pretty room! but there is a great hole in the floor now, and the ceiling is all tumbling down, and the table broken." [124]

"But why do you stay here?"

"Mamma and Emily say it is all the same. We are as safe in our cellar as we could be anywhere, and we should have to pay elsewhere."

"Then you cannot get out of Paris?"

"Oh no, while the Prussians are all round us, and shut us in. My brothers are all in the Garde Mobile, and, you see, so is my doll. Every one must be a soldier now. My dear Adolphe, hold yourself straight" (and there the doll certainly showed himself perfectly drilled and disciplined). "March—right foot forward—left foot forward." But in this movement, as may be well supposed, little Coralie had to help her recruit a good deal.

Lucy was surprised. "So you can play even in this dreadful place?" she said.

"Oh yes! What's the use of crying and wearying oneself? I do not mind as long as they leave me my kitten, my dear little Minette."

"Oh! what a pretty long-haired kitten! but how small and thin!" [125]

"Yes, truly, the poor Minette! The cruel people ate her mother, and there is no milk—no milk, and my poor Minette is almost starved, though I give her bits of my bread and soup; but the bread is only bran and sawdust, and she likes it no more than I."

"Ate up her mother!"

"Yes. She was a superb Cyprus cat, all grey; but, alas I one day she took a walk in the street, and they caught her, and then indeed it was all over with her. I only hope Minette will not get out, but she is so lean that they would find little but bones and fur."

"Ah, how I wish I could take you and her home to Uncle Joe, and give you both good bread and milk! Take my hand, and shut your eyes, and we will suppose and suppose very hard, and, perhaps, you will come there with me. Paris is not so very far off."

[126]

CHAPTER XVI.

THE AMERICAN GUEST.

"What can that be, coming at this time of day?"

Page 126.

No; supposing very hard did not bring poor little French Coralie home with Lucy; but something almost as wonderful happened. Just at the time in the afternoon, blind man's holiday, when Lucy had been used to ride off on her dream to visit some wonderful place, there came a knock at the front door; a quite real substantial English knock and ring, that did not sound at all like any of the strange noise of the strange worlds that she had lately been hearing, but had the real tinkle of Uncle Joe's own bell.

"Good morning. Where do you come from?"

Page 131.

"Well," said Mrs. Bunker, "what can that be, coming at this time of day? It can never [131] be the doctor coming home without sending orders! Don't you be running out, Miss Lucy; there'll be a draught of cold right in."

Lucy stood still; very anxious, and wondering whether she should see anything alive, or one of her visitors from various countries.

"There is a letter from Mr. Seaman," said a brisk young voice, that would have been very pleasant if it had not gone a little through the nose; and past Mrs. Bunker there walked into the full light a little boy, a year or two older than Lucy, holding out one hand as he saw her and taking off his hat with the other. "Good morning," he said, quite at his ease; "is this where you live?"

"Good morning," returned Lucy, though it was not morning at all; "where do you come from?"

"Well, I'm from Paris last; but when I'm at home, I'm at Boston. I am Leonidas Saunders, of the great American Republic."

"Oh, then you are not real, after all?" [132]

"Real! I should hope I was a genuine article."

"Well, I was in hopes that you were real, only you say you come from a strange country, like the rest of them, and yet you look just like an English boy."

"Of course I do! my great grandfather came from England," said Leonidas; "we all speak English as well, or better, than you do in the old country."

"I can't understand it!" said Lucy; "did you come like other people, by the train, not like the children in my dreams?"

And then Leonidas explained all about it to her: how his father had brought him last year to Europe and had put him to school at Paris; but when the war broke out, and most of the stranger scholars were taken away, no orders came about him, because his father was a merchant and was away from home, so that no one ever knew whether the letters had reached him. [133]

So Leonidas had gone on at school without many tasks to learn, to be sure, but not very comfortable: it was so cold, and there was no wood to burn; and he disliked eating horses and cats and rats, quite as much as Coralie did, though he was not in a part of the town where so many shells came in.

At last, when Lucy's uncle and some other good gentlemen with the red cross on their sleeves, obtained leave to go and take some relief to the poor sick people in the hospitals, the people Leonidas was with told them that he was a little American left behind. Mr. Seaman, which was Uncle Joe's name, went to see about him, and found that he had once known his father. So, after a great deal of trouble, it had been managed that the boy should be allowed to leave the town. He had been driven in an omnibus, he told Lucy, with some more Americans and English, and with flags with stars and stripes or else Union Jacks all over it; and whenever they came to a French [134] sentry, or afterwards to a Prussian, they were stopped till he called his corporal, who looked at their papers and let them go on. Mr. Seaman had taken charge of Leonidas, and given him the best dinner he had eaten for a long time, but as he was going to Blois to other hospitals, he could not keep the boy with him; so he had put him in charge of a friend who was going to London, to send him down to Mrs. Bunker.

Fear of Lucy's rash was pretty well over now, and she was to go home in a day or two; so the children were allowed to be together, and they enjoyed it very much. Lucy told about her dreams, and Leonidas had a good deal to tell of what he had really seen on his travels. They wished very much that they could both see one of these wonderful dreams together, only—what should it be?

[137]

CHAPTER XVII.

THE DREAM OF ALL NATIONS.

Oh! such a din!

Page 137.

What should it be? She thought of Arabs with their tents and horses, and Leonidas told her of Red Indians with their war-paint, and little Negroes dancing round the sugar-boiling, till her head began quite to swim and her ears to buzz; and all the children she had seen and she had not seen seemed to come round her, and join hands and dance. Oh, such a din! A little Highlander in his tartans stood on a whisky-barrel in the middle, making his bagpipes squeal away; a Chinese with a bald head and long pigtail beat a gong, and capered with a [138] solemn face; a Norwegian herd-boy blew a monstrous bark cow-horn; an Indian juggler twisted snakes round his neck to the sound of the tom-tom; and Lucy found herself and Leonidas whirling round with a young Dutch planter between them, and an Indian with a crown of feathers upon the other side of her.

"Oh!" she seemed to herself to cry, "what are you doing? how do you all come here?"

"We are from all the nations who are friends and brethren," said the voices; "we all bring our stores: the sugar, rice, and cotton of the West; the silk and coffee and spices of the East; the tea of China; the furs of the North: it all is exchanged from one to the other, and should teach us to be all brethren, since we cannot thrive one without the other."

"It all comes to our country, because we are clever to work it up, and send it out to be used in its own homes," said the Highlander; "it is English and Scotch machines that weave your cottons, ay, and make your tools." [139]

"No; it is America that beats you all," cried Leonidas; "what had you to do, but to sit down and starve, when we sent you no cotton?"

"If you send cotton, 'tis we that weave it," cried the Scot.

Lucy was almost afraid they would come to blows over which was the greatest and most skilful country. "It cannot be buying and selling that make nations love one another, and be peaceful," she thought. "Is it being learned and wise?"

"But the Prussian boys are studious and wise, and the French are clever and skilful, and yet they have that dreadful war: I wonder what it is that would make and keep all these countries friends!"

And then there came an echo back to little Lucy: "For out of Zion shall go forth the Law, and the word of the Lord from Jerusalem. And He shall judge among the nations, and shall rebuke many people; and they shall beat their swords into ploughshares, and their spears [140] into pruning-hooks: nations shall not lift up sword against nation, neither shall they war any more."

Yes; the more they learn and keep the law of the Lord, the less there will be of those wars. To heed the true law of the Lord will do more for peace and oneness than all the cleverness in book-learning, or all the skilful manufactures in the world.

FOOTNOTE:

[1] See the *Net*, June 1, 1867.

[1]

THE STANDARD SCHOOL LIBRARY.

(Each Volume, cloth, 50 cents. Sold singly or in sets.)

BAILEY. LESSONS WITH PLANTS. Suggestions for Seeing and Interpreting Some of the Common Forms of Vegetation. By L. H. Bailey. 12mo. Illustrated. xxxi + 491 pages.
This volume is the outgrowth of "observation lessons." The book is based upon the idea that the proper way to begin the study of plants is by means of plants instead of formal ideals or definitions. Instead of a definition as a model telling what is to be seen, the plant shows what there is to be seen, and the definition follows.

BARNES. YANKEE SHIPS AND YANKEE SAILORS. Tales of 1812. By James Barnes. 12mo. Illustrated. xiii + 281 pages.
Fourteen spirited tales of the gallant defenders of the *Chesapeake*, the *Wasp*, the *Vixen*, *Old Ironsides*, and other heroes of the Naval War of 1812.

BELLAMY. THE WONDER CHILDREN. By Charles J. Bellamy. 12mo. Illustrated.
Nine old-fashioned fairy stories in a modern setting.

BLACK. THE PRACTICE OF SELF-CULTURE. By Hugh Black. 12mo. vii + 262 pages.

Nine essays on culture considered in its broadest sense. The title is justified not so much from the point of view of giving many details for self-culture, as of giving an impulse to practice.

BONSAL. THE GOLDEN HORSESHOE. Extracts from the letters of Captain H. L. Herndon of the 21st U. S. Infantry, on duty in the Philippine Islands, and Lieutenant Lawrence Gill, A.D.C. to the Military Governor of Puerto Rico. With a postscript by J. Sherman, Private, Co. D, 21st Infantry. Edited by Stephen Bonsal. 12mo. xi + 316 pages.

These letters throw much light on our recent history. The story of our "Expansion" is well told, and the problems which are its outgrowth are treated with clearness and insight. [2]

BUCK. BOY'S SELF-GOVERNING CLUBS. By Winifred Buck. 16mo. x + 218 pages.

The history of self-governing clubs, with directions for their organization and management. The author has had many years' experience as organizer and adviser of self-governing clubs in New York City and the vicinity.

CARROLL. ALICE'S ADVENTURES IN WONDERLAND. By Lewis Carroll. 12mo. Illustrated. xiv + 192 pages.
CARROLL. THROUGH THE LOOKING GLASS AND WHAT ALICE FOUND THERE. By Lewis Carroll. 12mo. Illustrated. xv + 224 pages.

The authorized edition of these children's classics. They have recently been reprinted from new type and new cuts made from the original wood blocks.

CHURCH. THE STORY OF THE ILIAD. By Rev. A. J. Church. vii + 314 pages.

CHURCH. THE STORY OF THE ODYSSEY. By Rev. A. J. Church. vii + 306 pages.

The two great epics are retold in prose by one of the best of story-tellers. The Greek atmosphere is remarkably well preserved.

CRADDOCK. THE STORY OF OLD FORT LOUDON. By Charles Egbert Craddock. 12mo. Illustrated. v + 409 pages.

A story of pioneer life in Tennessee at the time of the Cherokee uprising in 1760. The frontier fort serves as a background to this picture of Indian craft and guile and pioneer pleasures and hardships.

CROCKETT. RED CAP TALES. By S. R. Crockett. 8vo. Illustrated. xii + 413 pages.

The volume consists of a number of tales told in succession from four of Scott's novels — "Waverley," "Guy Mannering," "Rob Roy," and "The Antiquary"; with a break here and there while the children to whom they are told discuss the story just told from their own point of view. No better introduction to Scott's novels could be imagined or contrived. Half a dozen or more tales are given from each book. [3]

DIX. A LITTLE CAPTIVE LAD. By Beulah Marie Dix. 12mo. Illustrated. vii + 286 pages.

The story is laid in the time of Cromwell, and the captive lad is a cavalier, full of the pride of his caste. The plot develops around the child's relations to his Puritan relatives. It is a well-told story, with plenty of action, and is a faithful picture of the times.

EGGLESTON. SOUTHERN SOLDIER STORIES. By George Cary Eggleston. 12mo. Illustrated. xi + 251 pages.
Forty-seven stories illustrating the heroism of those brave Americans who fought on the losing side in the Civil War. Humor and pathos are found side by side in these pages which bear evidence of absolute truth.

ELSON. SIDE LIGHTS ON AMERICAN HISTORY.
This volume takes a contemporary view of the leading events in the history of the country from the period of the Declaration of Independence to the close of the Spanish-American War. The result is a very valuable series of studies in many respects more interesting and informing than consecutive history.

GAYE. THE GREAT WORLD'S FARM. Some Account of Nature's Crops and How they are Sown. By Selina Gaye. 12mo. Illustrated. xii + 365 pages.
A readable account of plants and how they live and grow. It is as free as possible from technicalities and well adapted to young people.

GREENE. PICKETT'S GAP. By Homer Greene. 12mo. Illustrated. vii + 288 pages.
A story of American life and character illustrated in the personal heroism and manliness of an American boy. It is well told, and the lessons in morals and character are such as will appeal to every honest instinct.

HAPGOOD. ABRAHAM LINCOLN. By Norman Hapgood. 12mo.
Illustrated. xiii + 433 pages.
This is one of the best one-volume biographies of Lincoln, and a
faithful picture of the strong character of the great President, not
only when he was at the head of the nation, but also as a boy and a
young man, making his way in the world. [4]

HAPGOOD. GEORGE WASHINGTON. By Norman Hapgood.
12mo. Illustrated. xi + 419 pages.
Not the semi-mythical Washington of some biographers, but a clear,
comprehensive account of the man as he really appeared in camp,
in the field, in the councils of his country, at home, and in society.

HOLDEN. REAL THINGS IN NATURE. A Reading Book of Sci-
ence for American Boys and Girls. By Edward S. Holden. Illustrated. 12mo. xxxviii + 443 pages.
The topics are grouped under nine general heads: Astronomy, Phys-
ics, Meteorology, Chemistry, Geology, Zoölogy, Botany, The Hu-
man Body, and The Early History of Mankind. The various parts of
the volume give the answers to the thousand and one questions
continually arising in the minds of youths at an age when habits of
thought for life are being formed.

HUFFORD. SHAKESPEARE IN TALE AND VERSE. By Lois
Grosvenor Hufford. 12mo. ix + 445 pages.
The purpose of the author is to introduce Shakespeare to such of his
readers as find the intricacies of the plots of the dramas somewhat
difficult to manage. The stories which constitute the main plots are
given, and are interspersed with the dramatic dialogue in such a
manner as to make tale and verse interpret each other.

HUGHES. TOM BROWN'S SCHOOL DAYS. By Thomas Hughes.
12mo. Illustrated. xxi + 376 pages.
An attractive and convenient edition of this great story of life at
Rugby. It is a book that appeals to boys everywhere and which
makes for manliness and high ideals.

HUTCHINSON. THE STORY OF THE HILLS. A Book about
Mountains for General Readers. By Rev. H. W. Hutchinson. 12mo.
Illustrated. xv + 357 pages.
"A clear account of the geological formation of mountains and their
various methods of origin in language so clear and untechnical that
it will not confuse even the most unscientific."—*Boston Evening
Transcript.* [5]

ILLINOIS GIRL. A PRAIRIE WINTER. By an Illinois Girl. 16mo.
164 pages.
A record of the procession of the months from midway in September to midway in May. The observations on Nature are accurate and
sympathetic, and they are interspersed with glimpses of a charming
home life and bits of cheerful philosophy.

**INGERSOLL. WILD NEIGHBORS. OUTDOOR STUDIES IN
THE UNITED STATES.** By Ernest Ingersoll. 12mo. Illustrated. xii +
301 pages.
Studies and stories of the gray squirrel, the puma, the coyote, the
badger, and other burrowers, the porcupine, the skunk, the wood-
chuck, and the raccoon.

INMAN. THE RANCH ON THE OXHIDE. By Henry Inman.
12mo. Illustrated. xi + 297 pages.

A story of pioneer life in Kansas in the late sixties. Adventures with wild animals and skirmishes with Indians add interest to the narrative.

JOHNSON. CERVANTES' DON QUIXOTE. Edited by Clifton Johnson. 12mo. Illustrated. xxiii + 398 pages.
A well-edited edition of this classic. The one effort has been to bring the book to readable proportions without excluding any really essential incident or detail, and at the same time to make the text unobjectionable and wholesome.

JUDSON. THE GROWTH OF THE AMERICAN NATION. By Harry Pratt Judson. 12mo. Illustrations and maps. xi + 359 pages.
The cardinal facts of American History are grasped in such a way as to show clearly the orderly development of national life.

KEARY. THE HEROES OF ASGARD: TALES FROM SCANDINAVIAN MYTHOLOGY. By A. and E. Keary. 12mo. Illustrated. 323 pages.
The book is divided into nine chapters, called "The Æsir," "How Thor went to Jötunheim," "Frey," "The Wanderings of Freyja," "Iduna's Apples," "Baldur," "The Binding of Fenrir," "The Punishment of Loki," "Ragnarök." [6]

KING. DE SOTO AND HIS MEN IN THE LAND OF FLORIDA. By Grace King. 12mo. Illustrated. xiv + 326 pages.
A story based upon the Spanish and Portuguese accounts of the attempted conquest by the armada which sailed under De Soto in 1538 to subdue this country. Miss King gives a most entertaining history of the invaders' struggles and of their final demoralized rout; while her account of the native tribes is a most attractive fea-

ture of the narrative.

KINGSLEY. MADAM HOW AND LADY WHY: FIRST LESSONS IN EARTH LORE FOR CHILDREN. By Charles Kingsley. 12mo. Illustrated. xviii + 321 pages.
Madam How and Lady Why are two fairies who teach the how and why of things in nature. There are chapters on Earthquakes, Volcanoes, Coral Reefs, Glaciers, etc., told in an interesting manner. The book is intended to lead children to use their eyes and ears.

KINGSLEY. THE WATER BABIES: A FAIRY TALE FOR A LAND BABY. By Charles Kingsley. 12mo. Illustrated. 330 pages.
One of the best children's stories ever written; it has deservedly become a classic.

LANGE. OUR NATIVE BIRDS: HOW TO PROTECT THEM AND ATTRACT THEM TO OUR HOMES. By D. Lange. 12mo. Illustrated. x + 162 pages.
A strong plea for the protection of birds. Methods and devices for their encouragement are given, also a bibliography of helpful literature, and material for Bird Day.

LOVELL. STORIES IN STONE FROM THE ROMAN FORUM. By Isabel Lovell. 12mo. Illustrated. viii + 258 pages.
The eight stories in this volume give many facts that travelers wish to know, that historical readers seek, and that young students enjoy. The book puts the reader in close touch with Roman life.

McFARLAND. GETTING ACQUAINTED WITH THE TREES. By
J. Horace McFarland. 8vo. Illustrated. xi + 241 pages.
A charmingly written series of tree essays. They are not scientific
but popular, and are the outcome of the author's desire that others
should share the rest and comfort that have come to him through
acquaintance with trees. [7]

MAJOR. THE BEARS OF BLUE RIVER. By Charles Major. 12mo.
Illustrated. 277 pages.
A collection of good bear stories with a live boy for the hero. The
scene is laid in the early days of Indiana.

MARSHALL. WINIFRED'S JOURNAL. By Emma Marshall. 12mo.
Illustrated. 353 pages.
A story of the time of Charles the First. Some of the characters are
historical personages.

MEANS. PALMETTO STORIES. By Celina E. Means. 12mo. Illustrated. x + 244 pages.
True accounts of some of the men and women who made the history of South Carolina, and correct pictures of the conditions under
which these men and women labored.

**MORRIS. MAN AND HIS ANCESTOR: A STUDY IN EVOLU-
TION.** By Charles Morris. 16mo. Illustrated. vii + 238 pages.
A popular presentation of the subject of man's origin. The various
significant facts that have been discovered since Darwin's time are
given, as well as certain lines of evidence never before presented in
this connection.

NEWBOLT. STORIES FROM FROISSART. By Henry Newbolt.
12mo. Illustrated. xxxi + 368 pages.
Here are given entire thirteen episodes from the "Chronicles" of Sir
John Froissart. The text is modernized sufficiently to make it intelli-
gible to young readers. Separated narratives are dovetailed, and
new translations have been made where necessary to make the narrative complete and easily readable.

OVERTON. THE CAPTAIN'S DAUGHTER. By Gwendolen Overton. 12mo. Illustrated. vii + 270 pages.
A story of girl life at an army post on the frontier. The plot is an
absorbing one, and the interest of the reader is held to the end.

**PALGRAVE. THE CHILDREN'S TREASURY OF ENGLISH
SONG.** Selected and arranged by Francis Turner Palgrave. 16mo.
viii + 302 pages.
This collection contains 168 selections—songs, narratives, descrip-
tive or reflective pieces of a lyrical quality, all suited to the taste and
understanding of children. [8]

**PALMER. STORIES FROM THE CLASSICAL LITERATURE OF
MANY NATIONS.** Edited by Bertha Palmer. 12mo. xv + 297 pages.
A collection of sixty characteristic stories from Chinese, Japanese,
Hebrew, Babylonian, Arabian, Hindu, Greek, Roman, German,
Scandinavian, Celtic, Russian, Italian, French, Spanish, Portuguese,
Anglo-Saxon, English, Finnish, and American Indian sources.

RIIS. CHILDREN OF THE TENEMENTS. By Jacob A. Riis. 12mo.
Illustrated. ix + 387 pages.

Forty sketches and short stories dealing with the lights and shadows of life in the slums of New York City, told just as they came to the writer, fresh from the life of the people.

SANDYS. TRAPPER JIM. By Edwyn Sandys. 12mo. Illustrated. ix + 441 pages.
A book which will delight every normal boy. Jim is a city lad who learns from an older cousin all the lore of outdoor life — trapping, shooting, fishing, camping, swimming, and canoeing. The author is a well-known writer on outdoor subjects.

SEXTON. STORIES OF CALIFORNIA. By Ella M. Sexton. 12mo. Illustrated. x + 211 pages.
Twenty-two stories illustrating the early conditions and the romantic history of California and the subsequent development of the state.

SHARP. THE YOUNGEST GIRL IN THE SCHOOL. By Evelyn Sharp. 12mo. Illustrated. ix + 326 pages.
Bab, the "youngest girl," was only eleven and the pet of five brothers. Her ups and downs in a strange boarding school make an interesting story.

SPARKS. THE MEN WHO MADE THE NATION: AN OUTLINE OF UNITED STATES HISTORY FROM 1776 TO 1861. By Edwin E. Sparks. 12mo. Illustrated. viii + 415 pages.

The author has chosen to tell our history by selecting the one man at various periods of our affairs who was master of the situation and about whom events naturally grouped themselves. The characters thus selected number twelve, as "Samuel Adams, the man of the town meeting"; "Robert Morris, the financier of the Revolution"; "Hamilton, the advocate of stronger government," etc., etc.